P9-AGN-896

Weekly Reader Children's Book Club

A CLOCK FOR BEANY
HONEY

MAIL

WEEKLY READER CHILDREN'S BOOK CLUB presents

A CLOCK FOR BEANY

Story by Lisa Bassett • Pictures by Jeni Bassett

DODD, MEAD & COMPANY
New York

To our Mother

This book is a presentation of
Weekly Reader Children's Book Club.

Weekly Reader Children's Book Club
offers book clubs for children from
preschool through junior high school.
For further information write to:
Weekly Reader Children's Book Club
4343 Equity Drive
Columbus, Ohio 43228

Text copyright © 1985 by Lisa Bassett
Illustrations copyright © 1985 by Jeni Bassett
All rights reserved
No part of this book may be reproduced in any form
without permission in writing from the publisher
Distributed in Canada by
McClelland and Stewart Limited, Toronto
Printed in Hong Kong by South China Printing Company
1 2 3 4 5 6 7 8 9 10

Library of Congress Cataloging in Publication Data

Bassett, Lisa.
A clock for Beany.

Summary: Beany Bear is not quite sure he likes the clock he received for his birthday.
1. Children's stories, American. [1. Clocks and watches — Fiction. 2. Bears — Fiction] I. Bassett, Jeni, ill. II. Title
PZ7.B2933Cl 1985 [E] 84-13643
ISBN 0-396-08484-2

On Beany Bear's birthday a package came in the mail from Aunt Maud.

It was a clock.

Beany put it on the table next to his bed.

Beany's friend, Scamp Squirrel, brought him a jar of honey.

"Scamp, don't you think a little honey would taste good right now?" said Beany.

"Oh, no!" said Scamp. "We can't eat *now*."

"Why not?" asked Beany.

“Because it is not time for lunch,” said Scamp, pointing to the clock. “It is not twelve o’clock.” Beany looked at the clock and then at the honey. He was not sure he would like having a clock.

Finally, the hands of the clock were straight up. It was time to eat.

"I am ready for peanut butter and honey sandwiches," said Beany.

"Since it is your birthday," said Scamp, "I will make the sandwiches. Just leave everything to me. I will have lunch fixed in no time."

Scamp went into the kitchen.

Beany heard him making the sandwiches.

First he heard a bang, then a thump.

Suddenly there was a terrible crash.

"Don't worry," called Scamp. "That was only the honey jar."

"The honey jar!" cried Beany, rushing into
the kitchen.

"The *empty* honey jar," said Scamp. "I have
already made the sandwiches."

"Oh, I see—" said Beany.

"Throw the broken glass in the trash," said Scamp,
"and let's eat. You can clean up everything later."

That night, after Scamp had gone home,
Beany cleaned up the kitchen.
"I wish I had more honey," he said.
"But at least I still have my new clock."
Beany looked at his clock and saw some writing
on it. It said, "Push button to set."
Beany pushed the button. "There," he said,
"I guess that means I'm all set."

Early the next morning while it was still dark,
the clock began to ring with a loud *buzzzzz*.

"What is that noise?" cried Beany,
sitting up in bed and rubbing his eyes.
"Stop that buzzing!"

Beany thumped the clock, but it kept on buzzing.

He put the clock under his pillow, but he could still hear it.

When he plunked the clock into a glass of water, it just bubbled and buzzed.

"I won't get any sleep with a clock
in the house," cried Beany.
And he threw the clock out the window.
He crawled back into bed, but he could still
hear *buzzzzz* through the open window.

“I never knew clocks made so much noise,” growled Beany. He took his pillow and his blanket and stomped out of the house and into the woods. There he settled himself under a tree for a nice peaceful sleep.

Beany dreamed of golden pancakes dripping with honey. The dream was so real he could almost smell the honey.

Honey! He *did* smell honey! Beany opened his eyes with a start and sniffed the air.

"I've been sleeping under a honey tree!" he said. "That means bees! Bees will sting my nose!"

He jumped up to run away, but only went a few steps and stopped. There was something different about this honey tree. There were no bees.

Beany reached into the tree and licked up
the sweet, sticky honey. Not a bee was in sight.
"Oh, my! This honey is all mine!" he cried.
"I wonder how I could carry it all home."
Then Beany had an idea.

He tore open his pillow and sent the feathers flying.
He scooped up the honey and filled the pillow
until it was ready to burst at the seams.
Whistling cheerfully, he started off for home.

As Beany came down the path, he heard *buzzzzz* louder than ever. Just then he saw the clock. It was surrounded by a swarm of buzzing bees. "The buzz of that clock must have called the bees from their honey tree!" he cried.

Suddenly the clock made odd noises. It went *spling, buzz, ping*—and then it was silent. Beany saw the bees turn in his direction. “Oh, no!” he cried. “They must know I have their honey. Now I’m in trouble!”

But the bees took one look at Beany
and fled into the forest.
"What could have scared those bees?" Beany said.

When he went inside and looked in the mirror, Beany stopped and stared. Something strange was looking back at him.

"I hope I haven't turned into a monster," he said.

He put his pillow of honey in the kitchen
and went to scrub himself clean.

Then he looked in the mirror again.
"Oh, I'm glad I'm still me," he said.
"I don't think monsters like honey."

Beany began to pour the honey into jars. He poured and poured until the pillow was finally empty. Everything that could hold honey was filled to the brim.

Beany was licking his paws when a knock sounded at the door.

"Come in," said Beany.

"Is something wrong with your clock?"
asked Scamp. "I found it outside."

"It is broken," said Beany.

"Broken?" said Scamp. "Well, I know all about fixing clocks. Run get a hammer and I'll have it fixed in no time."

Beany paused. "A hammer," said Scamp. "Can't do a thing without a hammer."

Beany trotted off to get the hammer for Scamp.

"Now I'll show you just how we do this," said Scamp. He gave the clock a quick bang. The back part of the clock went flying into the air.

The front part of the clock went under the bed. All the little springs and wheels went all over the floor.

"There," said Scamp. "It is just as I thought.
There is something seriously wrong
with your clock."
Beany was inclined to agree.

"Be a good fellow and fetch the front part of the clock," said Scamp. "And then get a broom." Beany squeezed under the bed, while Scamp fished around in the sink. At last both the front and back parts of the clock were found.

"Now what?" asked Beany.

"Well, you have got to get this mess cleaned up," said Scamp. "I will keep working on the clock."

Beany swept the insides of the clock into a little pile and brought them to Scamp.

"Oh, just throw that junk away," said Scamp. "I have already finished. Yes, sir! You won't have any more trouble with this clock!"

"You don't think it will wake me up again?" asked Beany.

“Absolutely not!” said Scamp.

“You sure are good at fixing things, Scamp,” said Beany. “Look at the time. It is twelve o’clock!” He smacked his lips. “It is time to eat, and there is plenty of honey. Let’s make sandwiches.”

From that time on, Beany was very happy with the present from Aunt Maud. Whenever he looked at his new clock, it was *always* time for lunch.

Weekly Reader Children's Book Club